D1588422

MINI CLASSICS

SINBAD
THE SAILOR

RETOLD BY STEPHANIE LASLETT
ILLUSTRATED BY HELEN COCKBURN

SHOOTING STAR PRESS

TITLES IN SERIES I AND III OF THE MINI CLASSICS INCLUDE:

SERIES I

Aladdin and the Magic Lamp
Ali Baba and the Forty Thieves
Alice in Wonderland
A Child's Garden of Verses
Cinderella
The Emperor's New Clothes
The Frog Prince
Goldilocks and the Three Bears
Hansel and Grettel
The Happy Prince
The Little Mermaid
Mother Goose's Rhymes
The Owl and the Pussycat (and other Nonsense Verse)
Puss in Boots
Sleeping Beauty
Snow White and the Seven Dwarfs
The Town Mouse and the Country Mouse (and other
    Aesop's Fables)
The Three Little Pigs
The Ugly Duckling
The Wizard of Oz

SERIES III

Alice Through the Looking-Glass
Brer Rabbit's Riding Horse (and other Stories)
Brer Rabbit and the Turtle Race (and other Stories)
The Cat that Walked by Himself
The Elephant's Child (and How the Camel got his Hump)
The Fox without a Tail (and other Aesop's Fables)
The Golden Goose
Hush-a-Bye Baby (A Collection of Prayers
    and Lullabies)
The Little Match-Girl (and The Swineherd)
A Little Princess
Peter and the Wolf
Peter Pan
The Pied Piper of Hamelin
The Princess and the Pea (and The Red Shoes)
The Remarkable Rocket
Rumpelstiltskin
The Sorcerer's Apprentice
Tom Thumb
Wind in the Willows III – The Adventures of Toad
Wind in the Willows IV – Return to Toad Hall

© Parragon Book Service Ltd

This edition printed for:
Shooting Star Press, Inc.
230 Fifth Avenue-Suite 1212,
New York, NY 10001

Shooting Star Press books are available at special discounts for bulk purchases for sales promotions, premiums, fund-raising, or educational use. Special editions or book excerpts can also be created to specification. For details contact: Special Sales Director, Shooting Star Press, Inc., 230 Fifth Avenue Suite 1212, New York, New York 10001.

ISBN 1-56924-239-9

Printed and bound in Great Britain.

This is the story of Sinbad the Sailor and some of his strange adventures at sea. He travelled far and wide and each new voyage brought danger and excitement, as you will see!

His first voyage was on a merchant ship bound for the East Indies. It passed many islands along the way and stopped to trade with the natives. One day the ship was becalmed near a strange little island quite unlike any land the sailors had ever seen before. It was smooth and green and lay quite flat in the sea. The captain gave the crew permission to go ashore and soon they were stretching their legs on dry land. The cook had lit a fire and was preparing to make a meal when suddenly the island began to tremble and shake. The sailors still on board cried out in a panic.

"Quick! Run for your lives!" they shouted. "The island is moving!" But it was not an island after all. They had landed on the back of a whale and the heat of the flames had made him very cross indeed!

7

Quickly the sailors ran for
safety, some scrambling into
the sloop and some swimming
straight for the ship. The
captain raised his sail and as
soon as most of his sailors
were aboard, the ship weighed
anchor and was gone. But
Sinbad was left behind,
struggling in the swirling sea
as the great whale dived out
of sight. He clung to a piece of
driftwood and prayed to Allah
to save him from the dangers
of the deep. Soon darkness fell
and Sinbad passed the terrible
night in a daze.

Early the next morning Sinbad's prayers were answered for as the sun rose above the horizon he could see an island — a real island — and as the sun moved across the sky, the waves pushed him closer and closer to land until eventually he was thrown exhausted upon the beach.

This island was blessed with sweet spring water and plentiful fruit and so Sinbad survived for several days. But as time passed he feared he might never be rescued and would be doomed to spend the rest of his days lost and alone.

One day he resolved to explore the island fully and climbing to the top of a tall tree he scanned the island for signs of life. At first he could see nothing but sky, sea, sand and mile after mile of green forest but then his eye was caught by something white in the distance. Scrambling down from the tree he set off in the direction of this strange object. When he got close he saw it was a huge white dome, perfectly smooth but with no door or windows.

As Sinbad stared at it in wonderment, the sky suddenly grew dark and, lifting his head, he saw an enormous bird flying overhead. It was a Roc and the terrified sailor recalled how he had heard that this bird was so large that it fed its young on elephants!

The bird alighted upon the dome and Sinbad realised that it was her egg! As the Roc slept Sinbad had an idea.

"Maybe this Roc can help me escape from the island," he thought to himself and, unwrapping the turban from around his head, he tied himself securely to the bird's foot. All night long he waited for the bird to awake and at dawn she stood up and with a great cry took off into the sky. Higher and higher she soared, then suddenly swooped down and landed far below.

15

Hastily Sinbad untied himself and looked about. He was in a deep rocky valley surrounded on all sides by mountains.

"I will never escape from this dreadful place," he wailed. "Would that I had stayed on the island where there was at least food and drink to sustain me!" With a heavy heart he began to walk but had not gone far when he spotted something glistening on the ground. Bending down, he found to his amazement that the earth was studded with hundreds of glittering diamonds.

But as he admired their beauty, he saw something which struck fear into his heart. Watching him from the caves high above were many huge serpents, each one large enough to swallow an elephant in one go. They hid from the Rocs during the day and did not leave their caves, but at night they came down to catch what food they could find.

As the sun began to sink, Sinbad desperately searched for a place to hide. The serpents hissed loudly as they slithered down the valley towards him.

Quaking with fear, Sinbad crawled into a small hole and blocked the entrance with a rock. The terrible snakes hissed at him but could do him no harm. He was safe.

At sunrise the serpents slowly returned to their caves and Sinbad scrambled from his hole. As he stretched his cramped limbs, a huge piece of meat came crashing to the ground behind him. Down came another, and another. Then Sinbad remembered a story he had heard about diamond hunters. There was no way into the Valley of Diamonds and so they had devised a trick to bring the diamonds out. They threw lumps of meat down from the mountains onto the valley floor. The diamonds stuck to the moist flesh. Then eagles would swoop upon the meat and carry it to their nests in the mountains. Here the men lay in wait and, as soon as the birds had landed, they scared them away with sticks and could then safely pick the jewels from the meat. Sinbad realised the eagles could carry him out of the valley too.

Quickly he gathered as many diamonds as his pockets could carry and, once again untying his turban, he bound himself to the largest piece of meat and lay flat on the ground.

Straightaway an enormous eagle seized the meat with his talons and Sinbad found himself lifted into the air. The bird soared to the summit of a mountain and alighted on her nest. All at once a great hue and cry broke out and a man leapt out from behind a rock, waving a large stick. The frightened eagle dropped the meat and Sinbad speedily freed himself.

"What magic trickery is this?" cried the man when he saw a man but no diamonds. Then Sinbad described all that passed.

When Sinbad offered to share his own diamonds between them the man was most friendly and soon they were travelling to the city to exchange their gems for gold and silver.

After this, Sinbad returned home to Baghdad and great was the welcome, for his family had given him up for dead. So he passed several months in luxury and wanted for nothing, but after a time he longed for adventure once again. So, bidding his family farewell, he set sail on a merchant ship bound for distant shores.

The journey passed well enough for several months. The ship dropped anchor in the harbours of many fine cities and her merchant passengers did good trade and were well pleased. But their good luck was soon to end for one day a violent storm descended upon them and the tempestuous seas threatened to engulf them at any second. A great wind blew up and drove them off course and, when the gale had moved on, they could see an island rearing out of the sea straight ahead of them.

"Allah preserve us!" cried the captain and he fell to his knees on the deck. "That is the Island of the Ape Men. They are fearsome beasts and there will be no escape once they lay hands on us!"

Sure enough, Sinbad could see the creatures, half man, half ape, jumping up and down upon the shore. Suddenly they began swimming towards the ship and were soon crawling onto the decks and swarming up the rigging. They were covered with thick red hair and their eyes shone like yellow jewels.

The creatures could only grunt and bark and, as the captain beat his breast and cried aloud, they cut through the ship's ropes and cables with their sharp teeth.

When they were close to land, the Ape Men forced every sailor and merchant to swim ashore and, as Sinbad looked back, he was aghast to see that the wicked creatures had taken the ship and were quickly sailing away!

There was nothing for it but to explore the island and look for food and water. After many hours in the blistering heat they came upon a magnificent palace with high walls and tall spires. The huge ebony gates were ajar and so the exhausted group of men went inside, hoping to find kind hospitality. But the place seemed quite empty and deserted. Fires burnt under roasting spits in the courtyard and to one side was a huge mound of what looked suspiciously like human bones! The men were too tired to take another step so they sat down and rested. Suddenly the earth trembled and a dreadful roar filled the air.

A huge ogre lumbered through the gates and towered over the terrified men. So horrible was the sight that most of them fainted clean away on the spot.

The giant had one burning red eye in the middle of his forehead. His teeth were long and very sharp and his bottom lip hung down like a camel's. He had huge elephant ears and talons like an eagle. He was hideous.

When Sinbad came to, the first thing he saw was the ogre's huge eye just inches away from his face. To his great fear, he realised that the beast had him in his hand and was pinching him with two leathery fingers. The giant's fetid breath swept over him and Sinbad could hardly breathe. Then, with a short grunt of disgust, the ogre dropped Sinbad to the ground and picked up the captain. This time he let out a long rumble of pleasure, for the captain was nice and plump! He would have this one for his supper.

35

Soon the poor man was being roasted on a spit and as the others looked on in horror, the ogre ate him and tossed his bones on top of the large pile in the corner of the courtyard. Then, with much smacking of lips, the giant lay down on his back and slept, snoring loudly all the while.

The frightened men huddled together and spoke in whispers.

"We must escape!" said one.

"We must kill him!" said another, but no-one could agree on a plan.

"Listen to me," said Sinbad.

"We must make rafts and keep them on the shore so if we do not manage to kill the ogre then we at least have some means of escape off the island."

So it was agreed and they set to work immediately. The next evening the ogre once again picked a plump sailor for his supper but as he slept the men took two red-hot iron spits and thrust them into his one eye. With a great howl, the beast leapt to his feet and staggered out of the courtyard.

"He is not dead!" cried Sinbad. "To the rafts, to the rafts!"

38

They ran to the beach as fast as their legs could carry them and hastily pushed their flimsy rafts into the water. But who was this charging through the wood after them? It was the ogre — but he was not alone. He was accompanied by his wife, a giantess even more hideous than her mate. Roaring angrily, she picked up huge boulders as if they were pebbles and threw them into the sea, capsizing several rafts in one go. Soon the only sailors left alive were Sinbad and two companions.

The sea tossed them like a straw all through that dreadful night and the wretched men feared they would die at any time. But as the sun rose in the east they spied land and to their great joy the waves eventually threw them upon a sandy beach.

After walking some way, they congratulated themselves on their good fortune at having landed on an island with sweet water and ripe fruit and soon they were much restored in spirit and in health.

That night the three men slept upon the beach but were

wakened by a rustling sound coming towards them. Suddenly a great serpent reared over them and, darting forward, caught one of the sailors and swallowed him down. Sinbad and his one remaining companion quickly scuttled for safety.

"What misfortune is this!" wailed Sinbad. "We have escaped the cruelty of an ogre and the raging seas only to face this new and even more terrible danger." All that night the two men sat and shook but saw no more of the awful serpent. The following night they climbed into a tree.

"We will be safe from harm up here," decided Sinbad, but as the darkness gathered they could hear the serpent rustling towards them and with a great surge, he reared up from the ground and snatched Sinbad's companion from his branch.

The poor sailor was swallowed at once and the serpent slid away. Sinbad clung to the tree and trembled all through that long night.

The next morning he gathered as much dry wood as he could find and made himself a circle of small fires completely surrounding the tree. That night the serpent arrived as before but this time the flames kept him at bay. All night he lay in wait like a cat watching a mouse but at sunrise the hungry beast slunk away and Sinbad was safe once more.

The exhausted Sinbad could not face the prospect of another such night and so he ran to the beach, resolving to throw himself headlong into the sea and end all his troubles. But imagine his surprise and delight on seeing a ship pass by at that very moment! Unwinding his turban, he waved the bright cloth in the air and shouted at the top of his voice. Soon, to his great delight, the sailors had spotted him and turned the ship around. As Sinbad climbed aboard, the crew flocked about him, eager to hear his story.

They could hardly believe their ears when they heard that he had successfully escaped the dreaded cannibal ogre and his wife, not to mention the fearsome serpent. The captain welcomed him on board the ship and soon he had been fed and dressed in new clothes. As Sinbad rested, he overheard the captain giving instructions to one of the crew.

"When we disembark at our next port," he said, "be sure you do not unload these goods, for they belong to a sailor called Sinbad who we lost at sea many weeks ago. A huge whale has most likely swallowed him, but I wish to return his belongings to his bereaved family."

Then Sinbad leapt from his bed and hailed the captain. "It is I, Sinbad!" he cried. "Do you not recognise me? It was I who was left behind on that whale that we mistook for an island!" Then the captain embraced him and showed him the goods that he had kept safe and sound. And when they called at the next port, Sinbad increased his riches with wise purchases of cloves, cinnamon and other spices.

As they finally sailed for home they saw many wonders such as a tortoise twenty yards in length and a fish which looked like a cow and gave milk to its young.

And so after many months, Sinbad returned home, a prosperous merchant laden with fine goods, and his family were overjoyed to see him for they had long given him up for dead.

For several months Sinbad enjoyed the security and comforts of home, but as time passed, curiosity stirred within him and he longed to sail the high seas once again. Soon he was on board a merchant ship headed for the eastern isles with a fair wind in its sails. After a long, long voyage the ship finally arrived at a small island.

The ship's provisions were almost gone and the sailors and merchants had a fearsome hunger so the first thing they looked for was something to eat. Soon one of them gave a great cry. He had discovered a Roc's egg, similar in size to the one Sinbad had discovered on a previous voyage. As the crew gathered round, they could hear a faint tapping sound. Suddenly a crack rent the egg from top to bottom and the young Roc's bill appeared. Sinbad begged them not to touch the egg for he remembered the size of the mother Roc he had met before, and he feared they would be in grave danger if she returned, but the famished crew would not listen. Eagerly, the sailors attacked the shell and soon had the young Roc roasted upon a spit which they set up on the shore.

They fell on the meat like wolves as Sinbad sat to one side and watched them. Suddenly, he felt a shadow passing over him. Looking up, he saw the mother Roc flying high overhead, and close behind flew the enormous father Roc.

"Run for the boats!" cried the captain when he realised the danger they were in, and as the sailors scrambled hand over hand up the ropes, the ship set sail. Meanwhile the two Rocs had discovered their broken egg and no infant remaining. With anguished cries, they wheeled around and headed after the ship.

High overhead the Rocs circled and the sailors cowered beneath them on deck. Suddenly the huge birds flew off back to the island and a great shout of relief went up from the crew. But their joy was shortlived for soon the Rocs returned and this time each clasped a huge boulder in its talons.

With a triumphant scream, the Rocs dropped their burdens and they landed so exactly on the middle of the ship that it broke into a thousand pieces and every man on board was thrown into the sea.

Once again, poor Sinbad found himself clutching a spar of wood and counting himself lucky that he had not joined many of his shipmates who now lay at the bottom of the sea. One by one his companions drowned and Sinbad was the only survivor of that dreadful attack. Good luck continued to smile on him that day for soon a favourable wind got up and blew him towards a nearby island and as he lay gasping for breath on the sandy beach he gave thanks to Allah for saving his life once more.

This island too was blessed

with ripe fruit and pure water and soon Sinbad was much recovered in body and in spirit. He began to explore inland but had not gone far when he saw an old, old man, very weak and feeble, sitting by a brook.

"Hello, there," called Sinbad. "What country is this?" He got no reply from the old man who simply shook his head in a sorrowful fashion. After a while he raised his head and indicated that he wished Sinbad to carry him on his back over the brook so that he could gather fruit from the trees on the far side.

This Sinbad did gladly, for he was ever willing to help others less fortunate than himself. But when he got to the other side and bent down so that the man could step off his back, the old man simply gripped even tighter with his legs. He wrapped them so strongly around Sinbad's neck that he passed out and fell to the ground. Then the old man, whom Sinbad had thought so weak and sickly, gave him a mighty kick in the ribs and forced poor Sinbad to stumble to his feet and continue walking with the man still on his back.

And so poor Sinbad was little more than a beast of burden as the old man directed him from tree to tree. Steadily his new master ate his way through fruit after fruit and when night fell, the two slept locked together, with the old man's legs still gripped fast about Sinbad's neck.

In the morning, the bad-tempered old man kicked Sinbad awake and so the day's toil began again. Thus the week passed and poor Sinbad was desperate to rid himself of this troublesome burden. How he wished he had never stopped to do this good deed but he had no time to dwell on the matter for as soon as his steps faltered, the old man set about his head with his hands and there was no escaping his ill humour.

One day Sinbad spied a pile of empty gourds on the ground. While the old man slept, he carefully picked up a gourd, squeezed a quantity of grape juice into it and left it lying in the sun for several days. When he next returned to that place, he tasted the wine he had made and found it to be good and strong.

Soon he had a new spring in his step and his burden did not seem quite so heavy.

The miserable old man noticed the change in Sinbad's spirits at once and demanded to know what was in the gourd.

"It is wine, old man," replied Sinbad. "It gives me new strength and vigour." Then the old man was eager to taste it and Sinbad handed him the gourd. The old fool drank deep and soon he was dancing on Sinbad's shoulders and singing at the top of his voice. Needless to say, it wasn't long before he fell off!

Sinbad spotted his chance at once and took to his heels. Loudly the old man wailed as he realised the mistake he had made but Sinbad did not even look back over his shoulder.

Once again he roamed the shore, scanning the far horizon for a passing ship, and once again he was in luck. A heavily laden merchant ship picked him up and when they heard of his account of the old man, the sailors clapped him on the back.

"You had a lucky escape," the captain cried. "That is the old man of the sea and many men have died in his service. You are the first to ever escape his clutches."

So Sinbad was safe once more and after a good meal and the gift of some new clothes, he felt much restored. After some days had passed, a merchant on board the ship invited Sinbad to accompany him on a trip to a neighbouring island renowned for its coconuts. Each carrying a large bag, they set off for a grove of straight, tall trees with bark so smooth it was impossible for any man to climb up and reach their fruits.

The palm trees were alive with monkeys who chattered angrily at Sinbad far below. He was told to gather stones and then watched in amazement as the merchant threw the rocks at the monkeys. The creatures became incensed and grabbed the nearest missiles to hand — the coconuts. Soon coconuts were raining down around them and Sinbad quickly filled his bag.

This plan proved so effective that Sinbad eventually amassed a great pile of coconuts with which to trade at different ports. At each place they disembarked, he headed straight for the market and bartered for pepper and wood of aloes.

At one island he was shown the largest and most lustrous pearls he had ever seen. Hiring his own divers, he sat and watched while they fetched him shell after shell, each one concealing a hidden treasure.

So he returned home with more bounty and more tales to tell.

73

This time Sinbad rested for a full year before embarking once again on an adventure. He left a distant sea-port with a captain bound on a long voyage but after many weeks at sea the mariner declared that they were lost. Anxiously the crew scanned the horizon and when at last land was sighted, they were confounded by their captain's reaction. He fell to his knees, tore off his turban and beat his breast, calling loudly to Allah to save them all from the dreadful fate that surely awaited them.

"That is the most treacherous coastline in the whole of the Persian Gulf!" he cried. "We are caught in a rapid current and will be dashed upon the rocks. We are doomed, doomed!" Sure enough, the sailors seemed powerless to steer the ship away from the shore and soon the vessel ran aground and was broken into many pieces. The desperate sailors rescued what they could but were dismayed to find signs of many previous shipwrecks all along the coast. There was indeed no escape and one by one the men died.

Sinbad was the last to succumb to starvation and in desperation he hunted for a means of escape. He noticed that a channel of the sea ran some way inland and then disappeared underground.

"I shall follow its course," decided Sinbad, and he made a small raft. Carefully lashing his goods to the wooden spars, he climbed aboard and resigned himself to the will of Allah.

The current swept him along and soon the raft entered a dark cave. Sinbad lost all track of time as the hours passed in total darkness and silence.

The roof of the cave grew closer and closer and eventually Sinbad had to lie flat to avoid knocking his head on the overhanging rocks. As he lay tightly clinging to his goods, sleep overcame him and he knew no more.

When at last he awoke he was delighted to find that his surroundings had quite changed, for he was now amongst lush green fields. But then he saw that his raft had been moored against the river's edge and a group of natives stood watching him warily from the bank. None seemed able to understand him and at last in desperation Sinbad recited an Arabic prayer.

"Call upon the Almighty and he will help you. Shut your eyes and whilst you sleep, God will change your bad fortune into good." On hearing this, one of the men spoke out and welcomed Sinbad to their land. They offered him gifts of food and as he ate, he recounted the story of his voyage. They were most impressed and eager for him to repeat his story to their King at his palace in the city.

As Sinbad entered the city of Serendib, for that was its name, the people gathered around, curious to see this visitor to their small island.

He approached the King and bowing low before him, kissed the ground.

"My name is Sinbad," he said, "and I come from Baghdad." The King wished to know how he had arrived on the island of Serendib, and then Sinbad told the tale of all his voyages. The King was so entertained that he commanded that the adventures be written in letters of gold on vellum and kept forever in his library. Then Sinbad presented him with gifts from the goods he had rescued on his raft, and the King was well pleased by his generosity.

"You must take back a present from Serendib for your Sultan," decided the King and he dictated a letter to accompany the gift.

"To the Sultan, from the King of the Indies, before whom march a hundred elephants and whose palace shines with a hundred thousand rubies and twenty thousand diamond crowns."

When the time came for
Sinbad to leave, the King came
in great procession to the
harbour to say farewell. He rode
upon a magnificent elephant. A
palace guard walked in front of
him, carrying a long golden
lance, and another guard stood
upon the elephant's broad back
and carried a huge green
emerald upon a red velvet
cushion.

And so Sinbad set sail for his own country and as soon as he arrived in Baghdad, he went to the Sultan's palace to present the King of Serendib's letter and his gifts. The Sultan was much impressed by the generous presents, among which was a single ruby carved into a cup about six inches high and filled to the top with perfect pearls; a snake skin which had the power

to heal anyone who lay down upon it; bountiful quantities of wood of aloes and camphor; and a beautiful slave whose dress was covered in jewels. "I must reply to the King at once," declared the Sultan. "Sinbad, you will return to him with gifts from Baghdad."

Poor Sinbad had been hoping to spend some time recovering from his latest voyage but the Sultan would brook no delay and so a ship was loaded with costly presents from Arabia and Sinbad set course for the Island of Serendib.

Many days later he landed safely at the harbour, far away from the treacherous coast where he had been shipwrecked some months before. The King of Serendib welcomed Sinbad and was well pleased with the presents sent by the Sultan of Arabia. Happily he admired the beautiful coat made of gold cloth, fifty robes of rich brocade, yard upon yard of finest white linen, the magnificent carved table and the crimson velvet bed and at last he declared himself a great friend of the Sultan.

His task completed, Sinbad once again bade farewell to the Island of Serendib and set sail for home, but, alas, his journey was not to be a happy one. Four days from Serendib the crew were attacked by pirates and captured as slaves. On arrival at a neighbouring island, each rich merchant was stripped of his clothing and dressed in shabby rags, then sold to the highest bidder. Sinbad was bought by a local merchant who, luckily for him, treated him well. One day he called Sinbad to his side.

"Today you will go and shoot

elephants for me. Take this bow and arrow and do not return until you have killed at least one."

Then Sinbad was taken to a forest and made to climb a tree and lie in wait for the elephants to pass by. He spent the night without sleep but it was not until sunrise that the great beasts arrived. To Sinbad's great dismay, they sensed his presence and, surrounding the tree, stared at him with such malevolence that he almost fell from the tree in fright. Then the largest beast wrapped his trunk around the tree and pulled hard.

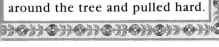

The tree toppled to the ground and Sinbad fell with it. He was plucked up by the elephant and slung on his back and, more dead than alive, was carried off to a low hill. There the animal left him alone and when Sinbad drew strength enough to look around he could see he was surrounded by the bones and tusks of countless elephants.

Sinbad knew at once that this was the elephants' own burial ground; the place they would come to when it was time for them to die. He realised that these wise animals had brought him here to show him that elephants should be allowed to die in their own time and not be hunted and killed simply for the ivory in their tusks.

Straightaway he returned to the merchant's house and explained what he had seen. When the merchant saw with his own eyes the remains of the hundreds of elephants who had died upon the hill, he was sombre.

"This is indeed an awesome sight," he told Sinbad. "I will take what ivory I can carry from this place and swear that I will hunt them no more." And so Sinbad loaded the elephant upon which they had come with many long tusks and then they returned to the merchant's house. The merchant was well pleased with Sinbad and as a mark of his appreciation he declared that he was no longer a slave but from henceforth could go free.

And so Sinbad returned home on his final voyage, for from that time on he never went to sea again. He had had great adventures and escaped danger and death more times that he cared to remember. He had survived mountainous seas, deadly rocks, hideous serpents and ogres, pirate attacks and all manner of strange afflictions. Now he wished to spend the rest of his days in the safe harbour of his house, tended by loving family and friends. After twenty seven years of travelling, Sinbad was home at last.

95

Sinbad the Sailor belongs to one of the greatest story collections of all time: *The Tales of the Arabian Nights*, also known as *The Book of One Thousand and One Nights*. These stories were first heard many hundreds of years ago and include *Aladdin and the Wonderful Lamp*, *Ali Baba and the Forty Thieves* and *The Magic Carpet*. The story goes that they were originally told by the beautiful Princess Scheherezade to the suspicious Prince of Tartary, who had threatened to behead her at daybreak. But her tales were so exciting that, as the sun rose, he longed to hear how they ended and so pardoned her life for one more day, until after one thousand and one nights Scheherezade had won his trust and his heart.